Christmas
at Grandad's Farm

by Claire Saxby

illustrated by Janine Dawson

The Five Mile Press

To the Dimboola crew

- Claire Saxby

For Wally, Peter and Laurie

- Janine Dawson

The Five Mile Press Pty Ltd
1 Centre Road, Scoresby
Victoria 3179 Australia
www.fivemile.com.au

Part of the Bonnier Publishing Group
www.bonnierpublishing.com

CIP data is available from the
National Library of Australia

© The Five Mile Press, 2013
Text © Claire Saxby, 2013
Illustrations © Janine Dawson, 2013
First published 2013
This edition 2014

Printed in China 5 4 3 2

Jingle bells, jingle bells
Jingle all the way,
Here we are on Grandad's farm
It's Christmas time. HOORAY!

At dawn on Christmas Eve
We're busting for a swim

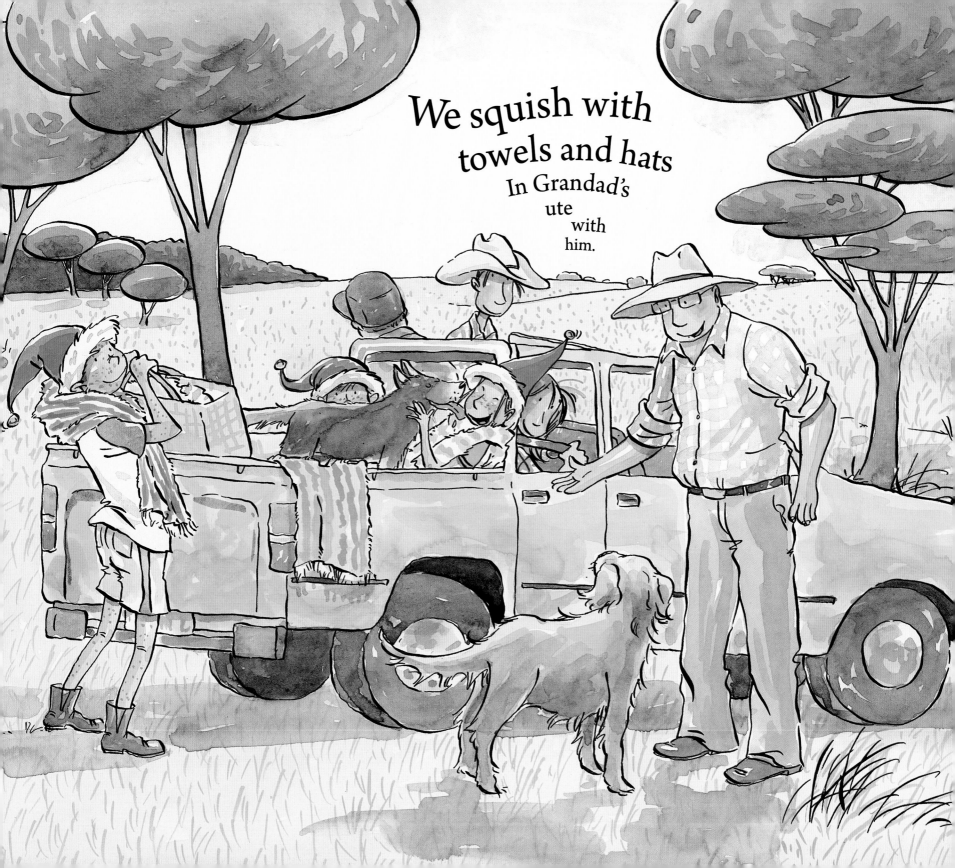

We squish with
towels and hats
In Grandad's
ute
with
him.

We drive along the creek
To our favourite swimming spot.

Dust clouds swirl so high around
They half-blind Uncle Scott.

Jingle bells, jingle bells
Jingle all the way,
Here we are on Grandad's farm
It's Christmas time. HOORAY!

Bashing through the dirt
In Grandad's yellow ute,
Over bumps we go,
Bouncing all the way.

Bells on red hats ring
As down the track we sway,
Oh, what fun it is to sing a
Christmas song today!

Oh, jingle bells, jingle bells
Jingle all the way,
Here we are on Grandad's farm
It's Christmas time. HOORAY!

The sun is shining bright.
The creek is cold and clear.

We ditch our shirts, our bells
And wade in up to here.

Our cousin swings up high
And lets go for the bomb.
The splash goes oh-so very wide
It drenches Dad and Mum.

Back at Grandad's place
We line up to be fed
Then Grandma scrubs us clean
And packs us off to bed.

Santa cannot come
Until we're all asleep.

We find it hard
to close
our eyes,
Even
counting
sheep.

Oh, jingle bells, jingle bells
Jingle all the way,
Here we are on Grandad's farm
It's Christmas time.
HOORAY!

Today is Christmas Day
And everyone is here,
We gather around the Christmas tree
To share the season's cheer

We scoff our Christmas feast

And play some family games

Then all pile into Grandad's ute
To swim the creek again.

Oh, jingle bells, jingle bells
Jingle all the way,

Here we are
on Grandad's farm

It's Christmas

time...

ZZZZZZZ